Just Kate

B. Grace Alford and Frances C. Milazzo

Archway Publishing books may be ordered through booksellers or by contacting:

Archway Publishing
1663 Liberty Drive
Bloomington, IN 47403
www.archwaypublishing.com
844-669-3957

Interior Image Credit: Frances C. Milazzo

ISBN: 978-1-6657-1623-9 (sc)
ISBN: 978-1-6657-1622-2 (hc)
ISBN: 978-1-6657-1621-5 (e)

Print information available on the last page.

Archway Publishing rev. date: 02/11/2022

To Our Granddaughters Skylar, Haley, and Kate. Always be who you are, because you are JUST AMAZING!

"Aahhhh!" Kamahele (kah-mah-HAY'-lay) sighed.
She had traveled for many days,
and she was so tired.
"Just a little bit farther," she said to herself,
"to the beach where I was born
twenty-five years ago."

Finally, her journey was done.

Kamahele paddled her way
across the sand, searching for the
perfect spot to lay her eggs.

"It must be far enough from the
waves that lap against the shore...

but not too far for my little ones
to walk when they are born."

"This is perfect!" Kamahele exclaimed,
and she began to dig her nest.

Using her back flippers, she dug out
a deep hole in the warm sand.

Kamahele laid 100 eggs—a very big family!

But she knew she would have to
leave her nest before sunrise.

"You will not be safe if I stay," she sobbed.

Then she said, "I will give each
of you a gift before I go.

My mother named me Kamahele,
which means 'traveler' in Hawaiian.
And I have traveled many miles.

So I will give each of you a special name
from a place in the world where sea turtles
roam. Your name will guide your destiny."

Kamahele patted each egg gently and
gave each one its own special name.

When she came to the last little round
egg, Kamahele said softly,

"You, my dear little one, I shall just name Kate.
Your destiny will be whatever you wish it to be."

With that, Kamahele covered up the nest
and walked slowly down to the water.

She turned only once to say a silent goodbye.

Sixty days and sixty nights went by.

Finally, on the night of a full moon,
a sound came from the nest.

Softly at first, then louder and louder . . .

Crack . . . *crack* . . . *crack!*

The baby turtles were hatching!

They popped out of their shells, blinking
their eyes rapidly in the bright moonlight,
shouting out their special names.

"Kaikoa!" (kai-KOH'-ah) shouted the first turtle as he energetically broke through his shell.

"My name comes from Samoa in the South Pacific, and it means 'sea warrior.'

I am the first to hatch, and so I am the eldest," he proclaimed with pride.

"Yuka!" (YU'-kah) exclaimed a girl turtle.

"My name is from the Aleutian Islands, way up north where waters are clear and cold. My name means 'bright star,' so I will be the one to light our way," she boasted.

Crack, crack, *crack!* Another baby turtle jumped up, waving his legs.

"Fernando!" (Fur-NAN'-do) he shouted. "My name comes from Baja California. And it means that I will be adventurous and brave."

On and on it went all night, until at last the final egg cracked, and out popped a joyful little girl turtle.

"Kate," she squealed in
a tiny, quiet voice.

Her brothers and sisters turned
toward her and laughed.

"Kate? Is that your whole name?
Just Kate?" scoffed Kaikoa.

"Why, yes," said Kate shyly. "Just Kate."

"But what does it *mean*?" asked Yuka.

"Yeah," said Fernando, "what is so
special about just Kate?"

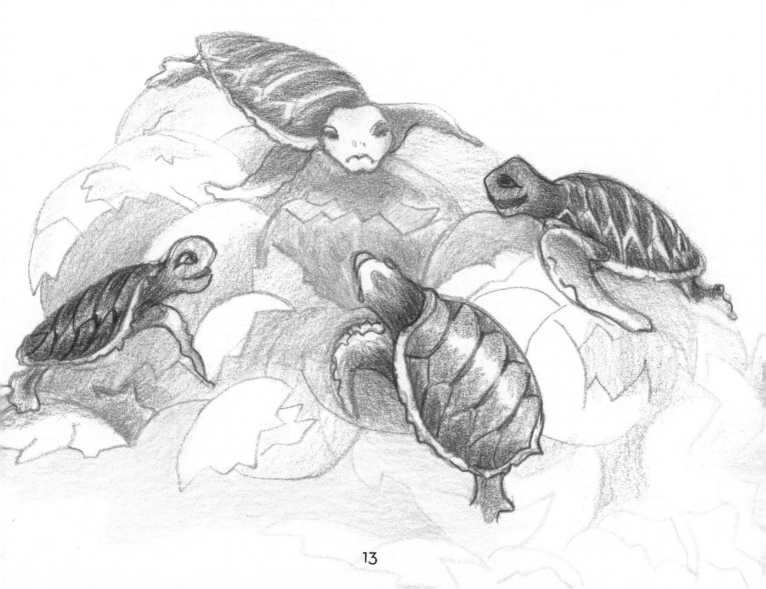

Kate did not know what to say.

"What *is* so special about my name?

Is there anything special about
me at all?" she wondered.

But Kate could not think about that for long.

All the baby turtles had to get to the water—fast!

"The light is this way!" hollered Yuka,
pointing toward the moon.

Fernando shouted, "Come on,
everyone; don't be afraid!"

Then Kaikoa gave a rallying call.
"Everybody—let's go!"

All the baby turtles
made a mad dash
across the dunes and
down the beach,
to the water's edge.
It was quite a sight!

Kate was the last to leave the nest, and she could see all her brothers and sisters in front of her.

"There they all go, with their special names," she said sadly.

"And here I am. Kate, just Kate." She sighed.

"What was my mother thinking giving me a name like that?"

At last resigned to her very plain name, she groaned, "Well, I guess I'd better get going too."

Kate saw the light of the moon beaming down on the water, and she knew that was the way.

She took a deep breath, dug her flippers into the sand, and started her run to the sea.

Just then, Kate heard Kaikoa scream.

A huge bird was diving right at him.
Kaikoa stared up in terror.

He wanted to run, but
his four tiny flippers
were frozen in fear.

Kaikoa knew he
was in trouble,
and Kate knew it too.

Suddenly, out of nowhere came Kate, scampering in front of the bird's path.

The diving bird shook his head. Seeing two turtles made him dizzy, and he dove straight down, missing them both— and giving Kaikoa time to escape.

"Whew, that was close!" exclaimed Kaikoa as he reached the water's edge.

A moment later, Kate glanced toward her sister.

Yuka was almost to the water,
but so was a giant crab.

He was red and mean, crawling sideways very
fast, clicking his claws, ready to attack.

"Look out, Yuka!" screamed Kate.
But Yuka did not hear her.

"He is *not* going to hurt my sister!" declared Kate.

Kate reached Yuka's side just in time to
send a flipper full of sand shooting right
into the crab's two bulging black eyes.

The sand made his eyes scratch and burn. And for a
moment, the crab could not see where he was going.

More importantly, he could not see Yuka.

It was just the right amount of time
for Yuka to get away too!

Kate was still shaking a little, but she
did not have time to be scared.

Adventurous Fernando had made it all the way to
the water when a big wave rolled in and turned
him over onto his back. There he was, helplessly
flailing his legs, with his hard shell pinned to the
sand. Waves rolled in over his head, making it
hard to see, or to move, or even to breathe.

Fernando was stuck!

"Someone has to help him!" Kate declared out loud.

She moved quickly to Fernando's side. Burying her sharp beak under his shell and pushing as hard as she could, she turned Fernando onto his belly.

Her brother looked down at his four feet on the sand and sighed with relief. "That's a *lot* better."

He gave Kate a quick wink and continued his march to the sea.

Kate helped as many of her brothers
and sisters as she could.

She nudged some of the slower turtles along, helped
others keep their balance in the deep sand, and
tried different tricks to scare away their enemies.

And somewhere along the way, Kate
realized she really liked helping.

It made her smile from the inside out.

It made her feel *special*.

"This is a feeling I want to keep forever!" she said.

It was almost morning, and Kate's work was done. So she stopped to rest.

A gentle breeze tickled her back, and Kate slowly opened her eyes.

"Oh. I guess it is time for me to go, too," she said, startled.

"Now just let me find that bright light."

Sleepy Kate spotted a yellow light shining
from a house overlooking the beach.

"Oh, there's the light. I need to go
that way," she told herself.

But it was the wrong light. *Kate
was going the wrong way!*

Kaikoa, Yuka, and Fernando were already in the water, and they turned around to see Kate marching farther and farther from the sea.

"Oh, no!" they gasped.

"If Kate does not turn around, she will be lost forever!" cried Yuka.

"Kate saved all of us. We must do something to save her!" Kaikoa said.

"Yes, but what?" asked Fernando, ready to help but not knowing what to do.

Suddenly, all three little turtles had the same idea at once.

The three nodded at one another and began
beating their flippers hard against the sea.

"Louder! Louder! *Louder!*" shouted Kaikoa.

They beat and beat until it sounded
like thunder on the beach.

Kate heard the noise and saw her sister and brothers splashing and waving. She quickly turned around and skittered as fast as she could toward the water.

"I'm almost there," she panted, nearly out of breath. Then with one last push of her back flippers, she plunged into the sea just ahead of angry diving birds, mean clicking crabs, and a very, very big wave.

When Kaikoa, Yuka, and Fernando saw
Kate in the water, they began to cheer.

Yay for Kate!
Yay for Kate!
Yay for Just Kate!

Kate was so happy. But in a few minutes,
the celebration was over. All the little turtles
swam off into the deep blue ocean.

Kate wondered if she would ever see Kaikoa,
Yuka, and Fernando again. The ocean was so big,
and there were so many places for turtles to go.

But no matter where they roamed, they would always remember the night they were born.

The night when they battled giant birds, mean crabs, and powerful waves to get safely to their ocean home.

It turns out their mother had given them the right names after all.

Kaikoa was a leader, Yuka was a guiding light, and Fernando was an adventurer.

As for Kate, her gift of helping others might have been the most important of all.

"I just *love* the name my mother gave me!" she declared with delight.

Being *Just Kate* was very special indeed.

TURTLE TRACK FACTS

* Green turtles can be found almost all over the world, but they like warm waters the best.

* Turtle mothers lay more than 100 eggs at a time.

* As soon as they are born, baby turtles must rush to the sea.

* Turtles spend most of their lives in the water, eating underwater plants and swimming thousands of miles.

* Their hard shells protect them from many enemies, but we need to do our part to help.

Author Biography

B. Grace Alford and Frances Milazzo are friends who grew up in Brooklyn, New York, together. While spending time in academic environments committed to the growth and development of children and teens, Barbara's career in Dothan, Alabama, has been focused on writing while Fran's professional pathway in South Huntington, New York, has been all about art. Their first book, *Just Kate*, was inspired by their experiences with their granddaughters.

CPSIA information can be obtained
at www.ICGtesting.com
Printed in the USA
BVHW022112140322
631491BV00006B/77